Homer

For porches—E. C.

Homer
Copyright © 2012 by Elisha Cooper
All rights reserved. Manufactured in China.
For information address HarperCollins Children's Books,
a division of HarperCollins Publishers, 10 East 53rd Street,
New York, NY 10022.
www.harpercollinschildrens.com

Watercolors and pencil were used to prepare the full-color art. The text type is Diotima.

Library of Congress Cataloging-in-Publication Data
Cooper, Elisha.
Homer / by Elisha Cooper.
p. cm.
"Greenwillow Books."
Summary: Homer the dog is content to watch from the porch
as his family goes out to enjoy the day.
ISBN 978-0-06-201248-7 (trade bdg.)
[1. Dogs—Fiction. 2. Human-animal relationships—Fiction.
3. Contentment—Fiction.] I. Title.
PZ7.C784737Hom 2012   [E]—dc23   2011013453

12 13 14 15 SCP 10 9 8 7 6 5 4 3 2 1   First Edition
Greenwillow Books

Homer

ELISHA COOPER

Greenwillow Books
An Imprint of HarperCollinsPublishers

Homer sits on the porch.

What does he want to do today?

Chase and race around the yard?

No, thanks.

Explore the field?

Thank you, but no.

Walk to the beach and play in the sand?

No, you go.

Swim in the waves?   Run to the market?

No, no. I'm fine right here.

The chasing and racing was very tiring!

Yes, I can tell.

The field was full of wind and flowers.

Mmm, sounds lovely.

The beach was beautiful, the sand was warm.

I can imagine.

The waves were big
and wild!

We got so many good
things to eat.

Oh, I'm so glad.

Do you need anything?

No, I have everything I want.

I have you.

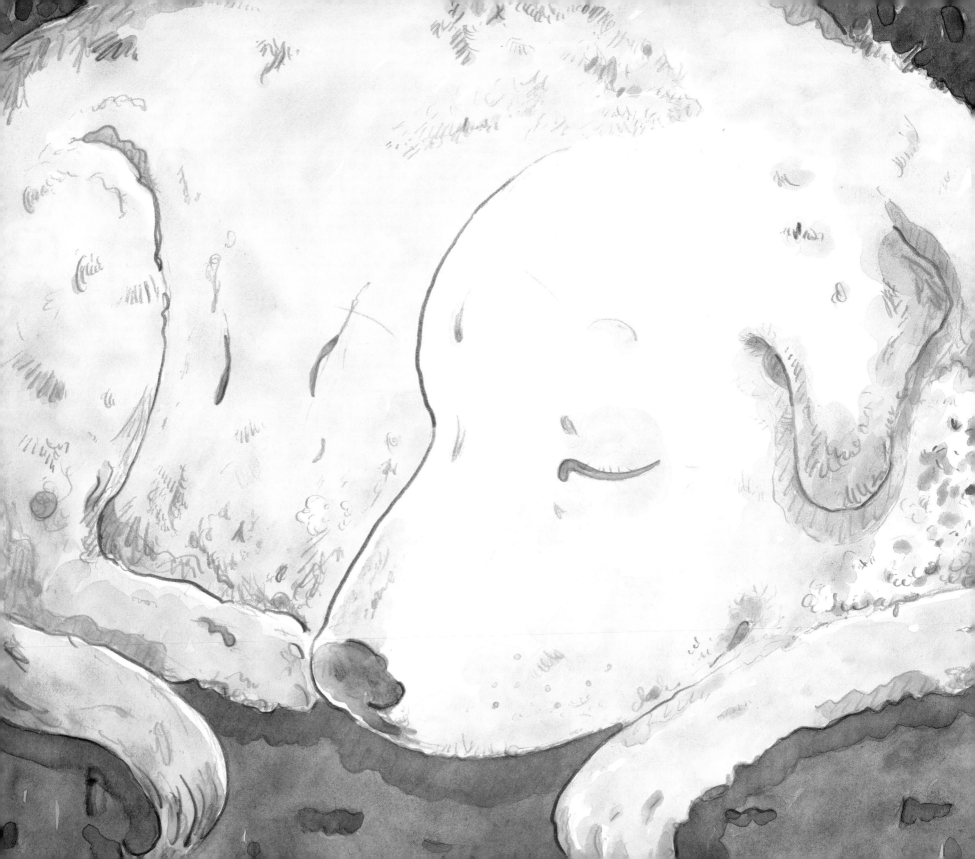